Ghostville Elementary®

Happy Boo-Day to You!

by Marcia Thornton Jones
and
Debbie Dadey

cover illustration by Guy Francis
interior illustrations by Jeremy Tugeau

A
LITTLE APPLE
PAPERBACK

SCHOLASTIC INC.
New York   Toronto   London   Auckland   Sydney
Mexico City   New Delhi   Hong Kong   Buenos Aires

To Susan Spain — What better friend could any person — or ghost — want?

— MTJ

To Danielle Kerr, Alexa and Bret Bergmeier, and Kyle Arenson — happy everyday to you!

— DD

No part of this publication may be reproduced in whole or in part, stored in a retrieval system, or transmitted in any form or by any means, electronic, mechanical, photocopying, recording, or otherwise, without written permission of the publisher. For information regarding permission, write to Scholastic Inc., Attention: Permissions Department, 557 Broadway, New York, NY 10012.

ISBN 0-439-56002-0

Text copyright © 2004 by Marcia Thornton Jones and Debra S. Dadey. Illustrations copyright © 2004 by Scholastic Inc. SCHOLASTIC, LITTLE APPLE, GHOSTVILLE ELEMENTARY, and associated logos are trademarks and/or registered trademarks of Scholastic Inc.

12 11 10 9 8 7 6 5   5 6 7 8 9/0

Printed in the U.S.A.   40
First printing, January 2004

Contents

THE LEGEND
Sleepy Hollow Elementary School
Online Newspaper

**This Just In: Spooky Sleepovers in
Sleepy Hollow!**

Breaking News: Late-night tales cause sleepless nights for students at Sleepy Hollow Elementary.

We've all heard eerie, hard-to-believe ghost stories. Maybe that's what caused four third graders to sneak back to school on Friday night. Were they looking to find ghosts? Or were they trying to get rid of one?

Stay tuned for more haunting news! Until then, sleep tight!

Your friendly fifth-grade reporter,
Justin Thyme

1
Party

"It's going to be the best birthday party ever!" Nina exclaimed, her dark eyes shining. "My *abuela* is making a piñata with candy and prizes hidden inside, and my mom said we can order pizza for dinner!"

"Hand me that red marker," Jeff snapped. He reached in front of Nina and grabbed a piece of paper.

Nina sat on the floor in the back corner of the classroom with her two best friends, Cassidy and Jeff. They were far away from the other groups. Nina was supposed to be helping Cassidy and Jeff draw a map of the seven continents. So far, Nina hadn't done anything except talk about her birthday party. She didn't

hand the marker to Jeff. She didn't even hear him.

"I've never been allowed to have a sleepover before," Nina said. "It's going to be great!"

As Jeff leaned over to snatch the marker from Nina, his black hair flopped down over his eyes. "How can it be great?" Jeff asked. "I won't be there."

Nina sighed. "I'm sorry, Jeff. I asked if you could come," she said. "Really, I did. But Mom said absolutely not."

"Why?" Jeff asked. "I thought your mother liked me."

"Of course she likes you," Nina said, "but this is a sleepover. It's only for girls!"

"If I had been invited, I could've brought the perfect monster movies to watch," Jeff told her. "Without me, your sleepover will be boring. How can a party be any fun if I'm not there?" he asked. Jeff was feeling left out, and he didn't like it one bit.

Cassidy slipped a loose strand of blond hair behind her ear. "Don't be mad," she told Jeff. "No boys were invited."

"Another reason why your party is destined to be boring," Jeff told Nina. "Everybody knows that boys are more fun than girls!"

Suddenly, a cool breeze rustled their papers. "Shh," Cassidy warned Jeff, "before we're overheard by you know who."

Soon after their third-grade class had moved into the basement, Cassidy, Nina, and Jeff had found out that the old

3

stories about a ghost class haunting the basement were true. It wouldn't have been so bad if the entire class could see the ghosts, but so far, the ghosts only allowed the three friends to see them. That meant that Jeff, Cassidy, and Nina had to keep the ghosts a secret. They knew that if they told their teacher, or even some of the other kids in their class, that they saw ghosts, they'd be sent to the school nurse — or worse.

Cassidy knew the ghosts liked to spy on them. They also had a habit of popping up when they were least expected. She tried to warn Jeff, but she was too late. A green haze swirled around the kids. The air sparkled like dust in a sunbeam. It grew heavier and thicker until the shape of a girl named Sadie formed before their eyes. No matter how often Cassidy watched the ghosts appear, it still sent goose bumps up her arms. Not Jeff, though. He thought it was cool.

"I wish I could come and go like that," Jeff said as they watched the ghosts take shape. "Then I could pop into your party whether or not I was invited."

A ghost named Becky floated over to Sadie. Two more shapes appeared. The kids recognized them right away as Ozzy and Nate. A pale ghost with a long braid and a big pink bow shimmered near the chalkboard. Her cat purred in her arms. Calliope and her pet, Cocomo, were new to the basement classroom.

Another ghostly form jumped between the kids, sending the map of the seven continents sliding across the floor. Huxley, Ozzy's dog, was always getting in the middle of things.

Sadie looked at Nina with big sad eyes. "Sleepover?" Sadie asked. "What is a sleepover?"

Nina knew Sadie was trying to be her friend. Nina looked around to make sure none of the other kids in her class were

watching. She didn't want them to think she had an imaginary friend. "A sleepover is when a bunch of kids get together to spend the night at one person's house. Didn't you ever have sleepovers?" Nina asked.

Becky shook her head. "Not unless you count the fact that entire families sometimes had to sleep in the same room."

"And that wasn't fun at all," Nate added.

"This isn't like that," Nina said. "Sleepovers are fun. They're an all-night party."

"Party?" Sadie asked.

"An all-night birthday party," Nina said. "For me!"

Sadie sniffed. She moaned and groaned. "Parrrr-tyyyy? I never had a party."

"Never?" Cassidy asked.

Becky tapped Nina on the shoulder. Well, at least Becky tried to, but she forgot to concentrate, which is what it takes for a ghost to actually touch something. Her hand went right through Nina's shoulder. Nina shuddered at the feeling of icicles on her skin.

"Most people in our town were poor," Becky explained. "Poor farmers. Poor shopkeepers. Poor, poor, poor."

"And Sadie's family was poorer than most," Ozzy whispered. "They never had money for extra things, like peppermint sticks, licorice, or fancy presents."

"It's a fact," Becky said. "Most of us didn't."

"I got a marble wrapped in butcher paper once," Nate admitted. "But I lost it the next day, and Pa told me I'd never get another."

"More," Sadie moaned. "Tell us more about your sleepover."

"Don't," Cassidy warned Nina.

But Nina was too excited to keep quiet.

2
Headless Ghost

Nina went on and on about sleepovers and how much fun the girls would have at hers. "We can stay up late and tell stories," Nina said, ignoring the map on the floor in front of her. "We'll laugh and tell jokes."

"I still can't believe you could have a party and not invite your best friend," Jeff muttered. "You really need me there. I'd spice up the party with a few good ghost stories."

"I know ghost stories that will scare the pants off you," a boy named Andrew said as he walked by the group.

Andrew was a big kid and didn't mind bullying anyone who got in his way. The ghosts swirled around his head as he plopped down on the floor next to the rest of the kids. Andrew didn't know the ghosts were there. Ghosts are like that. They are very picky about who they let see and hear them.

"Did you hear the story about the ghost without a head?" Andrew asked. "He wandered the streets, moaning, 'Where is my head? Whooooo toooook my head?'"

"That's sooooooo saaaaaaaad," Sadie moaned. "He must have been loooooonely."

Of course, Andrew didn't hear her. He also didn't see the other ghosts hovering above his head.

"How did the ghost see where he was going?" Nina asked, trying to ignore the five real ghosts that were buzzing around them.

"He wouldn't be able to see if he didn't have a head," Cassidy pointed out.

"Shh," Jeff told his two best friends. "This could make a good movie."

Cassidy couldn't believe Jeff was actually taking Andrew's side, even if Jeff's

11

favorite hobby was watching ghost stories. Jeff loved everything about scary movies and wanted to make them someday.

Andrew lowered his voice and leaned in closer. "Wherever the ghost went, people screamed and ran away. Well, that made this ghost downright mad. So he decided he needed another head."

"You don't just find heads lying around the supermarket," Cassidy said.

Andrew rolled his eyes. "Of course not. But this ghost was desperate, so he figured out a way to use a basketball as a head. And it worked for a while. He put on a long cape with a hood, and he was able to walk the streets, but only after the sun had set. No one seemed to notice, until one fateful night when a little kid wanted to ask him a question."

"What happened?" Jeff wanted to know.

"That little kid tugged on the cape, and when he did the head went . . . POP!"

When Andrew yelled the word and

grabbed at Nina, she shrieked and fell back against a desk.

"Got'cha," Andrew said with a snicker.

The kids' teacher, Mr. Morton, stood up from his desk and looked around the room.

"That wasn't funny, Andrew," Nina said as soon as Mr. Morton had gone back to grading papers.

"I thought it was hilarious," Andrew said as he got up from the floor. "Didn't you, Jeff?"

Jeff looked at Nina. He knew Nina hated to be scared, but he had to admit that Andrew told a good ghost story.

"These girls don't know how to have a good time like we do," Andrew told Jeff before heading back to his group. "Nighty-nightmares, girlie-girls!"

Suddenly, the air next to Sadie swirled like a tornado. Edgar, who usually spent his days writing stories in his journal, appeared. His wire-rimmed glasses slid down his see-through nose. "That was a goooood story," he said. "Truly brilliant."

Edgar's eyes lit up like two flashlights. He licked the end of his ancient pencil and started scribbling in his journal. Edgar loved spooky stories. The ones he wrote could scare the shells off eggs and the frosting off cakes.

"Your birthday party sounds like it would make the perfect setting for a story," he said. "I'll call it 'The Headless Ghost of the Sleepover Party.'"

Jeff leaned a little closer to Edgar and grinned. "Ghosts at a sleepover. You might be onto something," Jeff said. "In fact, that is the best idea I've heard all morning!"

Becky shook her head and backed

away. "If a scary story best describes one of those sleepover things, I'll have nothing to do with it," she said.

"My sleepover is definitely not going to be scary," Nina said. "It will be fun. Especially when I get to open my presents!"

"Will you get a shiny marble?" Nate asked.

"Or calico fabric to make a new dress?" asked Becky.

Nina giggled. "No. Presents nowadays are different. We get games, toys, and sometimes pretty things like jewelry."

Sadie suddenly pointed a long finger at the necklace hanging around Nina's neck. "Like the one I gave you?" she asked.

Nina had forgotten about the tiny heart dangling from a chain around her neck, even though it felt cold against her skin whenever Sadie was nearby. Nina had worn it every day since Sadie had given it to her. Nina knew that Sadie had been poor and that giving the necklace to Nina was truly a sacrifice.

Nina grinned at Sadie, remembering her pledge to try to be a good friend to the ghost. "Exactly," Nina told her. "And this is one of the best presents I've ever received."

Sadie smiled, which didn't happen very often, since 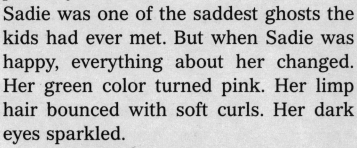 Sadie was one of the saddest ghosts the kids had ever met. But when Sadie was happy, everything about her changed. Her green color turned pink. Her limp hair bounced with soft curls. Her dark eyes sparkled.

Nina realized Sadie could be very pretty when she was happy. Nina silently made a promise to try to make Sadie smile more often.

But Sadie was the last person Nina was thinking about when she and the rest of the girls left school that afternoon. Nina was too busy thinking about her party to pay attention to anything else. She didn't notice Jeff muttering to Andrew. And she definitely didn't see Becky whispering in Sadie's ear.

3
Artemus Finnegan

"Happy birthday to me," Nina sang. "Happy birthday to me."

It was the evening of Nina's sleepover party, and she was in her family's big kitchen pouring lemonade. All of the girls from her class were downstairs. The fun had already started. Nina just knew this would be the perfect birthday party.

When she picked up the tray filled with glasses and turned for the steps, her foot got caught on the edge of a chair. Nina stumbled. The ice in the glasses clinked. The tray teetered in her grasp. Nina was sure the lemonade was going to spill everywhere, but at the last minute, the tray seemed to right itself, and Nina caught her balance.

"Whew," she said to herself. "That was a close call."

Suddenly, the tiny heart hanging around her throat felt like an ice cube and goose bumps scattered up her arms. Nina shivered and carried the tray of lemonade to her basement. She didn't spill one drop, even when she passed out the glasses to the girls.

"Let's play a game," Cassidy said after she took a big gulp of lemonade.

"How about . . ." Carla said slowly.

". . . pin the tail on the donkey?" Darla, her twin sister, suggested.

Cassidy nodded. It was a silly game, but who cared?

Everyone laughed when Carla pinned the tail on the donkey's nose. Darla ended up putting the tail on the donkey's ear.

Cassidy was sure she was heading to the right end of the donkey. When she pulled off the blindfold and saw the tail on the donkey's foot, she couldn't believe it. "You moved the poster," she yelled. "I know I had it right!"

A girl named Barbara shook her head. "No one touched that poster."

Barbara did even worse. Her tail wound up taped to the wall.

When Nina was blindfolded and twirled three times, she headed in the wrong direction, too. It looked like she was going to pin the tail on the couch. Carla giggled. Darla snickered. A few of the girls laughed out loud. Nina paused, and her free hand lifted the cold heart necklace away from her skin.

Suddenly, Nina swirled as if she had been turned around by invisible hands. Her outstretched hand reached toward the donkey's ears. Slowly, her arm moved along the poster until it hovered right where the tail needed to go. No one could believe it when Nina put the tail in exactly the right place.

"Have you been practicing?" Barbara teased.

Nina clapped her hands and did a little jump. "It was like magic. My hand just went that way."

"Spooky," a girl named Melissa said.

"That's it!" squealed a girl named Allison. "Let's tell ghost stories."

"They'd never believe the ghost stories we have to tell," Cassidy muttered to Nina as the girls turned off the lights and sat in a circle.

Carla leaned forward and started talking in a whisper. "Did you hear the one . . ."

". . . about Artemus Finnegan?" Darla finished.

The girls sitting in the circle shook their heads.

"I don't know if we should tell you," Carla said.

Darla nodded. "It's a story best forgotten."

"Tell us!" all the girls yelled at once.

Darla nodded. "Artemus Finnegan lived right here in our town of Sleepy Hollow. He did not have a single friend. Some say it was because his heart was as cold as a frozen river in winter. But the truth was that he was a greedy person. He wanted everything for himself and nothing for anyone else."

"He would snatch the last bit of left-over crumbs from a starving puppy rather than share them," Carla told them.

"No wonder he didn't have any friends," Nina said. "He sounds like a miserable person."

Darla nodded. "He *was* miserable. But he did find joy in his experiments."

"What kind of experiments?" Cassidy asked.

"He was determined to grow a new plant that could make him richer than the richest man on earth," Carla said. "He tried to grow bigger and juicier corn and bigger and sturdier wheat. Everything was bigger and bigger and bigger. That's what he tried to do."

"Was he successful?" Nina asked.

"The only thing he managed to do was attract spiders—lots and lots of them," Carla said. She looked straight at Nina when she said it. It was a known fact that Nina hated spiders. "It seems as though they liked the potions he used."

"What happened to Artemus?" Nina asked in a whisper, as if her own voice could wake the dead.

"Nobody knows for sure," Darla said. "Some believe his death was caused by the bite of a spider that had eaten one of his special potions."

"Others claim that Artemus was greedy even after his death," Carla said with a nod. "He still roams the streets of Sleepy Hollow in search of more riches."

"And wherever he goes," Darla whispered, so low that the girls had to lean forward to hear, "spiders follow!" Then Carla reached over and tickled Nina's knee.

"AAAHHHHH!" Nina jumped up and swatted Carla's hand away. The rest of the girls giggled.

Carla was laughing the loudest until she suddenly screamed. "Hey!" Carla yelled over the laughter. "Who pulled my hair?"

All the girls looked behind Carla. No one was there.

Cassidy looked at Nina. Nina held her locket in her hand as if she were trying to warm it up.

"Uh-oh," Cassidy whispered, but no one heard her. Nina jumped up and flipped on the lights.

"I've had enough scary stories," Nina said. She fingered the necklace around her neck. "Let's listen to music."

The other girls shrugged and started dancing to a CD, but Cassidy grabbed Nina's arm and pulled her aside. "I have

a creepy feeling that your sleepover is being haunted," Cassidy said.

Nina swallowed hard, and her face turned a sickly shade of yellow. "Do you think Artemus Finnegan is here?"

"No," Cassidy said. "I think one of our classroom ghosts has crashed your party."

"Don't be silly," Nina said. "You know the ghosts from Ghostville Elementary can't leave the school basement."

Cassidy shook her head. "I wish you were right, but remember when I broke my desk and Ozzy figured out that he could leave the basement as long as a piece of his old desk went with him?"

"Yes, but we hid that old piece of wood," Nina said. "And there is nothing else here that belongs to the ghosts." She looked over Cassidy's shoulder at the girls dancing in her basement. They were having so much fun. Nina wanted to dance, too. She didn't want to think about ghosts haunting her sleepover party.

"It's not the wood I'm worried about," Cassidy told her friend.

"Then what is it?" Nina asked.

Cassidy reached out and poked Nina's heart necklace. "This once belonged to Sadie. I think," Cassidy whispered, "a ghost traveled to the party with your necklace!"

4
Ghosts Just Want to Have Fun

"Impossible," Nina gasped. "It can't be."

"Yes, it can," Cassidy said. "Remember what happened when we brought that fiddle and the chipped dish from the Blackburn Estate and took them back to our classroom?"

Nina closed her eyes as if she were deep in thought. Then she slowly nodded. "We brought along two ghosts with them," she finally said.

"Exactly," Cassidy said. "Ghosts are forever stuck in one place — unless something that once belonged to them is taken from that very place. Then, and only then, can they leave. And you just happen to be wearing something that belonged to a ghost."

Nina shivered. "You're going to give me nightmares," she said. "But you just might be right. So where is Sadie?"

Nina and Cassidy looked around the room. The rest of the girls were hopping and twirling to the wild beat of the music. "There," Cassidy said, "next to Carla."

Nina squinted. Sure enough, the air seemed thicker next to Carla. When Nina looked closer, she saw Sadie dancing right beside Carla. Actually, Sadie floated in the air. She was trying to do the same moves that Carla was doing, but Sadie wasn't having much luck.

Carla turned and sent Sadie tumbling through the air until she landed halfway through the wall. Sadie popped out of the wall and tried another dance step. But when she tried to wiggle her hips like Barbara, Sadie ended up twisted like a corkscrew. Sadie looked ready to cry.

Nina rubbed her eyes. Could it be true? Could a ghost be in her very own modern basement? Nina made up her mind that when she grew up, she would never have a house with a basement.

Luckily, none of the other girls could see Sadie as she wiggled to the new dance, and they didn't hear Sadie moan when she couldn't get the steps right.

"She's not very good," Cassidy whispered. "I guess she's never danced like this before."

"At least she's trying," Nina said.

Cassidy nodded. "Poor Sadie. She's never been to a sleepover before. She just wants to be a part of the group."

"Let's do something else," Nina suggested to the rest of the girls. Nina didn't want to think about what a really mad ghost might do in her house.

"Let's fix each other's hair," Allison said.

"Jeff should be glad he isn't here," Cassidy said with a sigh as the girls paired up, leaving Sadie without a partner.

Sadie shrugged and pulled her own stringy hair up on top of her head. It looked like a bird's nest, and Sadie knew it. She pulled her hair until it stuck up wildly around her head. Tears the size of gumballs slid down her face and plopped on the floor by Nina.

Nina knew they'd better do something different and fast. "Let's paint our toenails," Nina said, holding up the present Barbara had given her. It was a huge set of twenty-five different bottles of nail polish. "Just be careful and don't spill any on the rug."

Cassidy chose lime green, and Nina

took bright pink. When all the other girls were busy painting their toes, Sadie concentrated hard so she could grasp a bottle of bright blue pol-ish. Sadie tried. But even though she concen-trated, the polish fell straight through her foot and landed on the rug.

"Look what you did," Carla blamed Darla when she saw the mess on the rug.

"I didn't do it," Darla snapped, wiping up the paint spots.

"It's right beside you," Carla accused her sister. "No one else is sitting there."

Thankfully, the doorbell rang to break up the fight, and Nina's mom brought down three boxes of pizza. "Get it while it's hot," her mom said, leaving the pizza for the girls.

"Yum," Cassidy said. "Pepperoni is my favorite."

Sadie floated over the pizza and breathed in the delicious smell. Unfortunately, Sadie also sent a chill over the pizza and turned it ice-cold. "Yuck," Barbara said, spitting out her bite. "This pizza is frozen."

"Don't worry," Nina said. "We can

warm it up in the oven. We'll watch a movie while we wait."

Later, while the girls were eating and watching the movie, Nina leaned close to Cassidy. "What are we going to do?" Nina whispered. "I wanted everything to be perfect. But how can I have fun when Sadie is so sad?"

Sadie was definitely not happy. She moaned and floated over the TV. Sobs echoed around the room. Sadie was so loud, Nina could barely hear the video.

"You have to think of a way to save my party," Nina said to Cassidy, "before it's ruined!"

Cassidy didn't have time to come up with a plan because just then, the lights went out and the TV went dead.

5
The Bogeyman?

"What's happening?" someone whimpered in the pitch-black basement.

"It's the end of the world," another voice said. She sounded like she was ready to cry.

Carla cried out. "It's the bogeyman . . ."

". . . and he's going to eat us all up," Darla added.

"No, he's not," Cassidy said. "There is no bogeyman. At least, I don't think there is."

Nina headed for the basement stairs. "I'll turn on the lights," she said, but she stopped short when she heard a screeching, scraping noise outside the door.

Carla was about ready to cry. "He's coming . . ."

". . . to get us!" Darla sniffled.

All the girls screamed and ran around, looking for a hiding place. "Nina's house is haunted!" Allison yelled.

Darla sat in the middle of the floor and started crying. "I want my mommy."

Above all the shrieking, Cassidy and Nina heard footsteps outside. Then something tapped against the window.

"It's Artemus Finnegan," Barbara screamed as she hid behind the couch.

"What if it's that headless ghost Andrew told us about?" Melissa cried from beneath the sleeping bag she had thrown over her head.

Nina was ready to faint. "The rest of

the Ghostville ghosts are here," she gasped, "and now everyone knows about them!"

"No, they don't," Cassidy said, her voice firm. "Nobody knows about the ghosts except you and me."

"And Jeff," Nina added.

"JEFF!" Cassidy blurted. "That's it! He didn't want to be left out so he decided to crash your party just like Sadie did."

"How can you be sure it's not Artemus Finnegan?" Nina asked.

"There's only one way," Cassidy said. She walked to the door that led outside. Step by step. Closer she went. She reached for the doorknob. The basement was silent as the rest of the girls waited.

"Don't do it," someone whispered into the darkness, but Cassidy didn't listen.

She grabbed the doorknob and tugged hard. Cassidy and Nina jumped outside just as two shadowy figures darted around the corner of the house, but not before Cassidy saw a baseball cap she knew only too well.

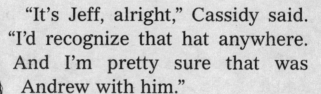

"It's Jeff, alright," Cassidy said. "I'd recognize that hat anywhere. And I'm pretty sure that was Andrew with him."

"You mean, we're being haunted by something worse than ghosts. We're being haunted by BOYS!" Nina said. "But why would Jeff want to ruin my party?"

"He doesn't want to ruin it,"

Cassidy said. "He just wants to be part of the fun."

"Why would Andrew help Jeff?" Nina asked.

"Jeff was mad about being left out of your party," Cassidy reminded Nina. "And Andrew never needs an excuse to cause trouble."

When Cassidy and Nina went back inside, the basement was filled with moaning. This moaning wasn't coming from Sadie. Now all the girls were in tears.

"Please stop crying," Cassidy said. "Nina's basement isn't haunted."

Carla put her hands on her hips. "If this isn't haunted . . ."

". . . then we don't know what is," Darla finished just as a huge *bang* came from the door and a window at the same time.

"Listen," Carla told her friends. The girls stopped crying long enough to hear footsteps outside the window.

"There really *is* someone out there," Darla yelled.

"Nina, call your mom! Call the police!" Barbara shouted.

Nina turned on a flashlight and shook her head. "We don't need to call anyone," Nina said firmly. "We're not going to be scared anymore."

"I'm scared," Darla whispered.

"Are you scared of Jeff?" Cassidy asked.

"Jeff?" the girls said together.

Cassidy nodded. "And Andrew. They're the ones making that noise."

"Those stinkers," Barbara snapped.

"And now that we're not scared," Cassidy said, "it's time to teach those boys a lesson."

6
Girl Revenge

Sadie flew through a chair to get in front of Nina. Nina waved Sadie away and looked at Cassidy. Hopefully Cassidy would have a good plan to get even with Jeff. They needed to do something really awesome. After all, this was revenge — girl revenge.

"Now," Cassidy said. "Does anyone have any ideas?"

The girls heard footsteps and some whispers from outside the basement window. Then there was a loud *clunk* against the glass.

"Are you sure it's only the boys?" Barbara asked.

"Positive," Cassidy said.

Everyone was quiet, but Sadie waved

her hands in front of Nina. "Not now," Nina told Sadie.

Barbara didn't understand that Nina was talking to Sadie. "We *have* to get even with Jeff *now*," Barbara said.

Sadie must have been worn out from flying around because she was definitely harder to see than usual. Still she managed to float in front of Nina's face.

"Will you please leave me alone?" Nina snapped at Sadie.

"Well," Barbara said in a huff, thinking that Nina had spoken to her. "You're the one who invited me to this rotten party."

"Oh, I'm sorry," Nina said. Her party *was* rotten and getting worse by the minute. Sadie buzzed around Nina's head until Nina felt like falling down from dizziness.

Nina shook her head, but Sadie wouldn't go away. Nina squeezed her eyes shut and hoped that Sadie would leave her alone for a few minutes. Nina needed to figure out how to handle this

boy disaster. But when Nina opened her eyes, Sadie floated right in front of her nose. Nina ducked away from Sadie and faced the other girls in the basement.

There was only one thing left for Sadie to do. She took a deep breath and concentrated with all her might. And then she broke the ghost sound barrier so everyone could hear. "I can help!" Sadie roared.

Barbara yelped. Melissa and Allison screamed.

Carla and Darla squealed. "Did you hear that?" they asked at the same time.

Cassidy quickly thought up a lie. "That must have been another one of Jeff's tricks." Then Cassidy grabbed Nina and nodded to Sadie. "The rest of you try to think of something while Nina and I check to make sure the bathroom window is locked."

Cassidy, Nina, and Sadie squeezed into the tiny basement bathroom. "What's your idea, Sadie?" Cassidy asked.

Sadie smiled and her skin changed from green to a rosy pink. Her hair shone and her eyes sparkled. Sadie leaned close to the girls and told them her plan.

7
Scared Senseless

"Sadie's idea is brilliant," Cassidy said. "We'll beat the boys at their own game."

Nina wasn't so sure. "What makes you think it will work?"

Nina and Cassidy stood by the side of the tub, their flashlight casting long shadows in the tiny bathroom. Sadie sat cross-legged in the air above the toilet. Her hair floated in a tangled mess around her face. Nina could barely see Sadie, but she figured it was because of the dim light from the flashlight.

"Jeff thinks he has us scared senseless," Cassidy explained. "The last thing he'll expect is for *us* to scare *him*!"

"But how will we make Sadie's plan work?" Nina asked.

"You do have a ghost," Sadie said. "A

real ghost. Me! Jeff doesn't know I'm here."

Nina smiled at Sadie. "It's nice of you to offer, but you couldn't scare a flea off a kitten. Jeff knows you, and he knows you're too nice. We need a bigger and much scarier ghost."

Sadie sighed. "A ghost like those Edgar writes about would do the trick," she said sadly. "I miss Edgar and Ozzy and Becky and Nate. And Huxley. Even Calliope and Cocomo would know exactly what to do."

Cassidy snapped her fingers. "We don't need them. What we need is the headless ghost of the sleepover party!" she said.

"If you could only make the headless ghost real," Sadie said.

Nina looked at Cassidy. Cassidy looked at Nina. They both looked at Sadie. "You are a genius!" Nina said.

"I am?" Sadie asked.

"A brilliant ghost genius," Nina said. "Follow us!"

Nina and Cassidy burst from the bathroom. The rest of the girls were huddled in a corner. An eerie scratching noise came from the window, but it stopped suddenly.

Carla whimpered. "Are the ghosts gone?"

"Did the haunting stop?" Darla added.

Nina smiled. "No," she said. "In fact, the haunting has just begun!" Then she told the rest of the girls their plan.

Nina liked sports, so it didn't take her long to gather the supplies they needed: the net off a soccer goal, two tennis rackets, a pair of stilts, football shoulder pads, a blanket, and, most important, a big orange basketball. While they worked, the girls heard Jeff and Andrew making noise outside. Every once in a while, one of the girls squealed to make the boys think the girls were actually scared.

When they were finished, even Carla giggled. "I think . . ."

". . . it just might work," Darla finished.

"All we have to do is trick them into walking into our trap," Barbara said. "And we'll be the bait!"

The rest of the girls hurried to take their places near the back door. Meanwhile Nina and Cassidy, loaded down with sports equipment, sneaked upstairs and out the front door. Sadie followed them. She had grown quiet, and Nina could barely see her, but the girls didn't have time to worry about Sadie. They had boys to trap.

Suddenly, the night erupted with screams.

"Help us!" Carla screamed. "It's the . . ."

". . . bogeyman," Darla yelled.

The rest of the girls came tearing around the outside of the house, pretending they were being chased by terrible monsters. Following in hot pursuit were Jeff and Andrew.

"Booga-booga-booga!" Andrew hollered.

"Booooooooooo!" Jeff added as the boys chased the girls around the corner of the house.

Jeff and Andrew both skidded to a halt. There, standing eight feet tall, was a creature from their worst nightmare. Its long white robe fluttered in the wind. Two giant arms reached out toward them. And then, before either boy could run, the creature's head fell off its broad shoulders and bounced right at their feet.

A green ball of flame shot up from the head and leapt at the boys. A horrible voice groaned, "I will get you!"

"Aaaaaahhh!" Andrew screamed.

"Aaaaaahhh!" Jeff screamed. "It's the headless ghost!"

8
Red-Handed

Cassidy jumped from behind a bush and threw the soccer net over Jeff and Andrew before they could escape.

"Caught you!" Carla sang out.

"Red-handed," Darla added.

All the girls danced around the trapped boys. Nina stood tall on her stilts, but she threw off the blanket and dropped her tennis-racket arms. Andrew and Jeff looked up at her.

"You tricked us!" Andrew sputtered.

"Yep," Nina said with a grin. "And you deserved it."

"You shouldn't have tried to scare us in the first place," Barbara added as the rest of the girls cheered in celebration.

Andrew's face turned red. So did Jeff's. They were even more embarrassed when Nina's mother and grandmother stepped out on the porch.

"*¡Los niños!*" Nina's *abuela* exclaimed.

Nina jumped off the stilts and stepped into the light that spilled from the open door. "The boys just wanted to wish me a happy birthday," she fibbed.

"Of course," Nina's mother said as she opened the door even wider. "Hello, boys. Please come in and join us for a piece of birthday cake."

As the rest of the girls filed inside, Nina turned to thank Sadie. "Sadie's green ball of flame was cool," Nina whispered to Cassidy, "but where did she go?"

"She's over there," Cassidy said, pointing to the shadows of the house.

Sadie wasn't taking part in the celebration. Instead, she hovered near a bush. Her sobs could barely be heard over the sound of the rest of the girls herding Andrew into the house.

"Sadie looks different," Nina told Cassidy. "Do you think she's okay?"

It was true. Sadie had grown very dim. Jeff untangled himself from the soccer net and came to stand by Cassidy and Nina. "How did Sadie get here?" Jeff asked.

As soon as Cassidy explained how Sadie had sneaked out of their classroom by traveling with Nina's necklace, Jeff figured out the problem. "She's losing her ghostly powers," he said. "Remember how the ghosts started to fade when they

tried to leave the basement to see the rest of the school?"

Nina shuddered and remembered when the ghosts had nearly disappeared completely. The ghosts had been so terrified that the kids had to help them. Nina knew she needed to help Sadie now. "What happens if she fades away?" Nina asked. "Will she be gone forever?"

"We can't wait to find out," Cassidy

said. "We have to help her get her energy back. Quick. Try giving the necklace back to her."

Nina rushed to Sadie and tried to put the necklace over the ghost's head. Sadie smiled at Nina and seemed to grow a bit brighter. But when the necklace fell through her body, Sadie started crying again.

"We may be too late," Cassidy whispered to Nina and Jeff.

"I want my friends," Sadie moaned. "I don't belong here. I tried, but I just don't belong." The more Sadie cried, the dimmer she grew.

"You need to go back to school," Nina said. "You need to be with your ghost friends."

Sadie sniffled. "I don't know how," she

said. Then she started crying so hard she nearly faded completely.

"You have to take her back there," Jeff said to Nina and Cassidy, "before it's too late."

"Will you help us?" Nina asked.

Jeff crossed his arms over his chest. "I'm sure you don't need my help," he called over his shoulder as he followed Nina's mom into the house for cake.

"I can't believe Jeff is still mad because I couldn't invite him to my party," Nina said.

"We can't worry about Jeff right now," Cassidy said. "Sadie needs our help."

Nina nodded. "Jeff's right," she said. "It's up to us."

Cassidy tried to calm Sadie. "We'll help you, but we have to wait until everyone is asleep," Cassidy said.

"I only hope," Nina said, "that it won't be too late."

9
Cemetery

After Andrew swallowed his cake and gulped his juice, he turned to Jeff. "Let's go," Andrew grumbled. "There are too many girls around here for me."

Jeff thanked Nina's mom and *abuela* and followed Andrew out the door. Nina grabbed Jeff's arm and whispered, "Aren't you going to help us take Sadie back to school?"

Jeff shrugged. "You didn't want me at your sleepover, so you don't need my help."

"That's not true," Nina said. "I wasn't allowed to invite you. You're a boy!"

Jeff didn't hear her. He had already followed Andrew out the door. After the boys left, Nina and Cassidy hurried the rest of the girls to their sleeping bags.

When they were sure everyone was asleep, Nina and Cassidy sneaked out the back door. Sadie slowly followed. By now, she was only a glimmer.

"If we don't hurry, Sadie may be lost forever," Nina whispered to Cassidy.

The street was dark and deserted. Long shadows reached across the sidewalk, and a chill wind rustled tree branches. Dried leaves and twigs crunched under the girls' feet, sounding like bones cracking. "We have to take the shortcut," Cassidy told her friend. "It's the only way we'll get back in time."

Nina knew exactly what shortcut Cassidy meant. It was the one through Sleepy Hollow Cemetery. "There has to be another way," Nina said with a whimper. "Maybe we'll make it in time if we run."

Cassidy pointed at Sadie. "Sadie won't be able to keep up with us if we run. She's too weak."

Nina swallowed hard. "Okay. Then I

guess we'll have to go slowly through the cemetery," she finally said.

The cemetery stood between Nina's neighborhood and the school. The girls slipped through the gate and made their way down the narrow lanes of the grave-yard. It was scary enough in broad day-light. In the dead of night, it was worse than creepy. Gravestone shadows reached out toward the girls like long, bony fin-gers. Leaves crunched under their feet, and somewhere, an owl hooted. As Cassidy swept the beam of her flashlight from side to side, Nina was sure she saw something scuttling out of their way. Sadie's moaning didn't help, either.

Once Sadie lifted her hand like she was waving to someone. Nina shivered. She didn't want to think about who or what Sadie might be waving to.

The three girls were halfway through the cemetery when Cassidy's flashlight lit up an old headstone sitting in a tangled web of vines. A crack zigzagged down its center, and green moss grew inside the engraved lettering.

Nina paused to look at the writing on the stone. "HERE LIES ARTEMUS FINNEGAN," she read out loud. "A MEANER MAN NEVER LIVED."

"How terrible," Cassidy said.

"This was the man your friends spoke of," Sadie said faintly as she settled down to rest upon the tombstone. "The one who fed the spiders as well as his own greed."

If there was one thing Nina hated, it was spiders. She could just imagine them crawling all over her. "Let's get out of here," Nina yelped as she scratched her arms and legs, and even her belly button.

The girls were in such a hurry to escape from Artemus Finnegan's grave that they didn't pay attention to where they were going. They wandered around graves and pushed through brambles. They tripped

HERE LIES
ARTEMUS
FINNEGAN

A MEANER
MAN NEVER
LIVED.

over roots that looked like skeleton feet and ran from statues that looked like monsters waiting to pounce.

Finally, Cassidy pulled Nina to a stop when they passed a gardening shed for the third time. "We're lost," Cassidy said with a gulp.

Sadie hovered near them, her shape so faint that she could barely be seen.

"What are we going to do?" Nina cried.

Just then, a huge form jumped out from behind the old shed and shouted, "BOO!"

10
Boo

"Aaaaahhhhhh!" screamed Nina as she tumbled backward into a pile of leaves.

"Aaaaahhhhhh!" screamed Cassidy as she tripped over a clump of roots.

"Ohhhhhh, nooooooo!" moaned the ever-fading Sadie as she somersaulted through the air.

Was it a monster? Was it a ghost? Was it the bogeyman? No, it was worse than that. It was Andrew and Jeff.

"That was not funny," Nina said, brushing leaves from the seat of her pants.

Andrew laughed out loud. "If you had seen the looks on your faces, you wouldn't be saying that," he said.

"He's right," Jeff said. "It was funny."

"What are you two doing in the cemetery, anyway?" Cassidy asked.

"Following you," Andrew said matter-of-factly. "What are *you* doing here? Shouldn't you be at your party?"

Nina and Cassidy had to think up a lie, and quick. "We're having a spelling bee at my sleepover," Nina said.

"We need our spelling books so we know what words to use," Cassidy added. "And our books are at school."

Andrew looked at Nina as if she had just grown polka-dot fur, but Jeff knew exactly what was happening. He glanced at Sadie. She wasn't crying her usual sobs. She was too weak to moan and groan. Instead, she whimpered. Jeff also noticed how dim she was growing.

"We need that spelling book in a hurry," Nina said, reading Jeff's mind. "But we got all turned around, and now we don't know which path takes us out of here."

Andrew laughed wickedly. "This is even better than I'd hoped for. Come on, Jeff," he said. "Let's leave these girls to

rot in the ceme-
tery."

"No!" Cassidy
said. "You have
to help us."

"No, we don't,"
Andrew said.
"Do we, Jeff?"

Nina put her
hand on Jeff's
shoulder. "I'm sorry you weren't invited
to my party, but this is serious."

Jeff looked at his friends. They had left
him out of the party, and he didn't know
if he could forgive them. But when Jeff
looked at Sadie, he knew exactly what
he needed to do. If Sadie didn't get back
to the basement soon, she would disap-
pear forever. He knew he would feel
awful if that happened. "Quick," he said,
"follow me."

"Hey!" Andrew called as Jeff took off.
"You're ruining all the fun! Come back!"

Andrew stood by himself as Cassidy

and Nina disappeared down a path after Jeff. Branches rattled over Andrew's head, and something scurried through the leaves by his feet. When a puff of wind blew against Andrew's face, he was sure he distinctly heard the word "boo."

"Hey!" Andrew yelled. "Wait for me!"

11
Puff of Smoke

The kids were panting by the time they made it to Sleepy Hollow Elementary. They stopped at the dark stairway that led down to their basement classroom and waited for Sadie to catch up. Inside the building, Jeff saw a dim light burning. "Olivia must be working late," he said.

"Or maybe she's putting a ferret to bed," Nina said.

Olivia had been the janitor at Sleepy Hollow Elementary since before the kids were even born. Nobody knew much about her except for one thing: Olivia was always helping animals.

"We have to be quiet so Olivia doesn't know we're here," Jeff said. "She can't find out about the ghosts."

Sadie held her head in her hands as she floated toward the kids. She had grown so faint that they could barely see her. She looked like a mist ready to be blown away by the wind. Sadie no longer cried, moaned, groaned, or even whimpered. "My friends," she sniffed. "Where are my friends?" Sadie sounded worse than sad. She sounded scared.

"What do you think happens to ghosts when they fade away?" Cassidy whispered.

Jeff shrugged. He usually acted like he knew everything there was to know about ghosts. Not tonight. "It's never happened in any of the movies I've seen," he said.

"I don't want her to fade away forever," Nina said. "Sadie only wanted to be my friend. She only wanted to be part of the party."

"I happen to know exactly how she feels," Jeff said, "but right now, we have to get her inside. It's her only chance."

"Maybe Olivia left the classroom door unlocked," Cassidy said, disappearing down the dark back stairway that led to their classroom.

Nina gulped. "Don't go," she told Cassidy, but Cassidy had already been swallowed up by the thick blackness.

Nina started to panic as she stood at the top of the crumbling steps with Jeff and Sadie. In the moonlight, Sadie barely made a green glimmer.

"Rats," Cassidy said, clomping back up the steps. "It's locked."

Sadie moaned as a breeze blew through her. Now, only her face was visible in the moonlight.

"We have to do something fast," Jeff said.

"I have an idea," Sadie whispered. Her voice was almost lost in the night air.

Before Sadie could tell them her idea, Andrew raced across the playground and tackled Jeff. "What's the big idea leaving me stranded in the cemetery?" Andrew asked.

Jeff pushed Andrew away. "Get over it," Jeff said. "We have a job to do."

But as the three kids turned back to Sadie, she disappeared like a puff of smoke.

"She's gone!" Nina yelped.

"Who?" Andrew asked.

"We have to do something!" Cassidy said.

"About what?" Andrew wanted to know.

"Maybe Ozzy can help," Jeff suggested.

"Who's Ozzy?" Andrew asked.

Jeff acted like he didn't hear Andrew and raced down the steps. "Help me," Jeff called over his shoulder. Cassidy pulled Nina down the stairs.

"Knock as hard as you can," Jeff said. "We have to get the others to help us."

The three kids knocked. They pounded. They beat on the door. Andrew stood at the top of the steps and stared down at them all.

"Becky! Ozzy! Nate! Edgar!" Jeff yelled. "Open up!"

Suddenly, the door flew open, and Cassidy, Jeff, and Nina fell inside. The three kids looked up and up and up at a huge form blocking the doorway.

"It's Artemus Finnegan!" screamed Nina.

12
Spooky Disaster

"Oh, no!" Cassidy yelped.

Jeff held up his hand and tried to think of something to say. His mind was blank. Even Andrew, who usually had something smart-alecky to say, was speechless.

Nina was the only one brave enough to speak. She knew she had to speak up to help Sadie. "Hello, Olivia," Nina whispered.

"Fancy meeting you kiddies out this late," Olivia said.

A big crow sat on Olivia's shoulder and squawked. Olivia laughed so hard, her earrings jingled and the keys on her belt jangled. Or maybe her earrings jangled and her keys jingled. "I think you young-uns have been listening to too many ghost stories. Imagine mistaking me for

Artemus Finnegan. Why, he was much better looking than me." Olivia laughed again, and the crow echoed, "Caw, caw, caw!"

Nina felt a shiver run down her spine as Sadie reappeared beside her. "Get into the school," Nina whispered, but it was no use. Sadie was too weak to move. Nina felt like crying. They had come all this way for nothing. But then a slight breeze gave Nina an idea.

"Blow," she told her friends. Jeff, Cassidy, and Nina blew like they were trying to put out a forest fire with their mouths. Andrew didn't know what was happening, but he blew anyway. Nina couldn't feel Sadie anymore. Had she disappeared again?

"What are you kids doing here, and why are you breathing all over me?" Olivia asked. The crow on her shoulder flapped his wings, adding to the wind made by the kids.

Nina blew one last time and smiled.

Behind Olivia, the kids saw a faint green glow growing stronger and brighter. Nina knew that Sadie would be all right now that she was back home.

Jeff found his voice and squeaked, "We wanted to borrow a spelling book."

"And we're out of breath from running the whole way," Nina added.

"A little late-night spelling test?" Olivia asked. "Maybe you should start by spelling *trouble*."

Cassidy nodded. "I think we just changed our minds. Didn't we, Nina?"

Nina nodded. She hoped they wouldn't get in too much trouble for being out so late. What would her mom and *abuela* say if they found out?

Her spooky sleepover hadn't ended the way Nina had planned, but at least Sadie was safe. Even if she was a ghost, Sadie was still a friend, and friends were what parties were all about.

Nina smiled. Maybe her birthday party had been a success after all.

13
A Real Party

"Now, this is what I call a party," Jeff said after he had taken a whack at the piñata. He barely dented the side, but Jeff didn't care. He still had fun. It was a few days after the sleepover, and the kids were back in their third-grade classroom. Nina had helped her *abuela* make another piñata, and her mother had even made cupcakes for Nina's school birthday party.

Nina laughed because the classroom ghosts had gotten into the act. They were punching the piñata with their fists. Andrew lifted his blindfold and stared at the piñata. He couldn't see the ghosts and he couldn't figure out what was making the piñata spin around.

Andrew shook his head, pulled down

his blindfold, and swung at the piñata with a broomstick. He made a slight crack in the side. Ozzy laughed. He flew up to the ceiling before diving headfirst into the piñata. *Pop!* The piñata exploded. Candy and ghosts filled the air.

"Awesome!" Carla and Darla squealed as they scrambled for candy. All over the classroom, kids filled their pockets with treats. The ghosts even managed to steal some away to a back corner. Nina was glad to see Sadie looking healthy — as healthy as a ghost can look. Huxley, the ghost dog, happily licked a candy wrapper beside Cocomo, the ghost cat.

"Thanks for bringing the piñata," Mr. Morton told Nina. "It was a nice treat."

Nina smiled and winked at Sadie. "This is the way parties are supposed to be," Nina said. "All my friends are together, and we're having fun. What more could a kid want?"

Sadie floated by and giggled. "What more could a ghost want?"

Ready for more spooky fun?
Then take a sneak peek at the next

Ghostville Elementary®

#7 Hide-and-Spook

The next morning, Jeff, Nina, and Cassidy met in their classroom before school started. A cloud of dust floated in the weak sunlight filtering through the dirty classroom windows. A new cobweb draped from Mr. Morton's desk to the file cabinet. The air smelled a bit like dirty socks. But that's not what bothered Cassidy.

"Are you okay?" Jeff asked. "Did you see a new ghost?"

Cassidy shook her head. She opened her mouth to speak, but no sound came out. Instead, she pointed to her desk. There, sitting in her seat, was the old doll from the 1800s. And it was looking straight at her.

"Andrew is just teasing you again," Nina said.

When Cassidy finally spoke, her voice squeaked. "It's not Andrew," she said. "I hid that doll in the coat closet after Andrew left school yesterday."

"Then he must have snuck in later," Jeff said. "This time, we just have to hide that doll someplace Andrew will never think to look."

Before Cassidy could say "hocus-pocus," Jeff had snatched the doll and carried it out of the classroom. Nina and Cassidy followed him down the hall. "Andrew will never think to look here,"

Jeff said as he opened a storage closet and stuffed the doll behind a box.

As soon as the kids closed the door, the air in the hallway turned so cold they could see their breath. A green cloud of glitter swirled around their heads. That could mean only one thing—ghosts.

Ozzy and Becky popped up in front of them. Ozzy peered over their heads. Becky looked around their backs.

"Is she gone?" Becky asked.

"Good riddance, I say," Ozzy said.

"Who?" Nina asked.

"You know who," Becky said. She pointed a finger at Cassidy and sniffed. "You had better be careful. That's all I have to say."

"Becky is right," Ozzy added. "With *her* around, there is bound to be nothing but trouble."

And then Ozzy and Becky disappeared like bubbles popping.

"What was that all about?" Jeff asked.

"Who were they talking about?" Nina wanted to know.

Cassidy didn't say a word. She had a terrible feeling she knew exactly who they were talking about. And if the ghosts were afraid, then she knew one thing: They should all be afraid. Very afraid . . .

And don't miss these spooky tales

Ghostville Elementary®